# BUG EYED MONSTERS

## JEAN URE

A & C Black • London

First published 2012 by
A & C Black, an imprint of Bloomsbury Publishing Plc
50 Bedford Square, London WC1B 3DP

www.acblack.com
www.bloomsbury.com

ISBN: 978-1408-1-5267-6

A CIP catalogue for this book is available from the British Library.

This book is produced using paper that is made from wood grown
in managed, sustainable forests. It is natural, renewable and
recyclable. The logging and manufacturing processes conform to the
environmental regulations of the country of origin.

Printed by CPI Group (UK), Croydon, CR0 4YY

3 5 7 9 10 8 6 4 2

# BUG EYED MONSTERS

## JEAN URE

# CONTENTS

# CHAPTER ONE

# A STAFFROOM FULL OF ALIENS

'Pass it on… Mr Snitcher isn't human!'

'Pst! Mr Snitcher isn't human!'

'Mr Snitcher… he's not human!'

Nobody ever knew where the rumour first came from. Harry heard it from his best friend, Joe Fredericks. Joe heard it from Andy Bicknell, standing in the lunch queue. Andy got it from his cousin, who got it from a boy in Year 7, who got it from his brother, who was in Year 8. Andy didn't say where the brother got it from. Not that it mattered. It was the second week of term, and people were ready for a good story.

'Hear about the Snitch? He's not human!'

It wasn't the first time there had been rumours of extra-terrestrials at St Bede's. Back in Year 4, when Harry had just started, Joe had solemnly informed him that there were aliens on the teaching staff.

'Dunno who, exactly, but we reckon there could be a whole nest of 'em.'

Looking at the teachers, Harry had been quite prepared to believe it. What a bunch! Any single one of them could have come from another planet.

There was Mr Bulstrode, the science teacher, who spat when he got excited. Splattered huge distances, right from the front of the lab to the back. Baljit Singh had once taken an umbrella in with him.

'Don't want to get wet, sir!'

Mr Bulstrode had stared up at the ceiling in surprise.

'Have we sssprung a leak, then?'

Baljit said, 'No, sir,' (dodging spit), 'it's just a precaution, sir.'

'Strange boy,' mused Mr Bulstrode.

He thought *Bal* was strange? How about Mrs Jellaby, the art mistress, otherwise known as Mrs Jellybaby? Mrs Jellybaby *looked* like a jellybaby. She was immensely round, and soft, and squishy, and so strung about with great ropes of beads and bangles that when she went shopping she had to use the supermarket trolley to take some of the weight.

Fact! She had been seen, walking the aisles of the local Tesco, with her great jangling necklaces resting on top of a bunch of toilet rolls.

'Reckon she'd have overbalanced, otherwise!'

Then there was Mr O'Hooligan, the PE teacher, who slept upside down every night, hanging off his bedroom door like a bat.

Also fact. Piers Allan, in Year 7, swore to it. Piers had actually been climbing up the drainpipe at the time, trying to sneak back into his dorm before anyone discovered he was missing, and had just happened to stop on the way and peer in at Mr O'Hooligan's window.

'Upside down, he was, like a bat!'

And how about Mr McNutter, the woodwork teacher, who stuck pencils in his ear and then forgot about them? Or Monsieur Tittinbot, who taught French and had a glass eye, which sometimes fell out when he grew agitated? Once when it fell out it had rolled across the floor, and Monsieur Tittinbot had screamed at the boys not to trample on it.

'*Attention, attention*! Beware of the eye!'

Even the Head, Dr Dredge, a long thin man like a length of rubber tubing, was not above suspicion. Dr Dredge was so very long, and so very bendy, that he was able to twist his arms and legs into strange knots, all tangled up together, so that he looked as if he were made of elastic.

Furthermore, he could bend his thumbs back until they touched his wrists. He did this frequently, sitting there in morning assembly, in front of the whole school, bending his thumbs and twisting his legs, winding them round like strings of spaghetti.

What normal human being could do that?

Joe had a theory — Joe had theories about everything — that the entire staff was probably made up of extra-terrestrials, with Dr Dredge at the head.

'He'll be the mastermind... the one behind it all. World domination,' said Joe, darkly. 'That's what they're after.'

Rumours came, and rumours went. As one died down, another started up.

The next one, Harry remembered, had been about Mr Potts.

'Hey! Guess what?'

Poor old Pudgy Potts had been abducted by aliens! They had come, and they had taken him.

Without a shadow of a doubt, Mr Potts had disappeared. There one day, gone the next. The official explanation was a nervous breakdown.

'Caused, I do not doubt,' spat Mr Bulstrode, 'by the loutish behaviour of some of you boys. Baljit Ssssingh, why are you holding a book over your head?'

'Just taking cover, sir,' said Bal. 'Sir, are you absolutely certain, sir, that Mr Potts has had a breakdown?'

'What elsssse,' hissed Mr Bulstrode, 'would you ssssuggest?'

'We thought he might have been abducted by aliens, sir.'

'A likely tale!' scoffed Mr Bulstrode.

Well, it wasn't very likely, of course. No one really took it seriously.

Still, it was funny how the rumours persisted. Aliens on the staff – teachers being abducted – Mr Snitcher not being human.

'Word! The Snitch ain't human!'

Rumours didn't come from nowhere.

Joe still reckoned that Mr Snitcher wasn't the only one. 'I reckon there's hordes of 'em!'

The others weren't so sure. It was a nice idea, but… why choose St Bede's?

'Seems to me,' said Joe, 'a school's exactly what they would choose. Plant a few aliens in with the teachers, who'd know the difference?'

'Should have thought they'd go for somewhere a bit more important,' said Bal. Bal had a bit of a tendency to argue. 'Like the Houses of Parliament, or somewhere.'

'Parliament's probably already full of 'em,' said Joe. 'Whole country's probably overrun by now.'

It was only a game, of course. They all accepted that; even Joe. Nobody really believed the country was overrun by aliens. The Houses of Parliament, maybe; but the whole country? That was felt to be pushing it.

On the other hand, Mr Snitcher not being human… well! That was a different matter. That really might be true. As Ryan said, he certainly didn't look human. What he looked like, more than anything, was an alien trying to blend in and not quite succeeding.

What human being ever had a body that was so thin and twiglike? So covered in knobbly bits? With a face that was so froglike, and eyes that were so bulgy?

'Bug eyes,' said Joe. 'Sure sign.'

As for his ears…! They flapped on either side of his head like giant pancakes in the breeze. Sometimes, when he was taking class, he would pull one of his ears forward so that it almost wrapped round his cheek.

'Antennae,' said Joe, tapping the side of his nose. 'Needs 'em for picking up extra-terrestrial signals.'

But then there was his name: Snitcher. Would an alien really choose a name like that?

Joe, as always, had a theory. He said it was precisely the sort of name an alien *would* choose.

'Obviously he liked the sound of it… obviously appeals to an alien ear.'

They considered it, the four of them, as they lay in bed in the dormitory after lights out.

'You don't reckon,' said Bal, at last, 'that he'd go for something a bit more ordinary, like Smith or something?'

'Nah!' Joe dismissed the suggestion with an airy wave of the hand. 'Dead give-away. Anyone calls themselves Smith, you know at once it's not their real name.'

There was a silence.

'My auntie's called Smith,' said Ryan.

'Yeah?'

'Yeah.'

'Your auntie an alien?'

Carefully, Ryan said, 'I don't think so.'

'There you are, then.' Joe lay down, with a satisfied thump. 'That proves it!'

No one was quite certain exactly what it was that had been proved, but you didn't argue with Joe. He had an answer for everything.

'Guess we could always try asking the Fish,' said Harry.

'Ask the Fish? What for?' Joe shot back up again, immediately suspicious. Was Harry daring to question him? 'I already told you, Smith's what people choose when they want an alias.'

'Alien alias,' said Bal. He chortled. 'Hey, that's really difficult to say! Alie*nay*lias. Ali- '

'Do you mind?' said Joe.

'I was just saying! Alie*nay*lias. Ali- '

'Thought we could pick his brains,' said Harry.

'About what?'

'About how you might recognise one. An alien, that is.'

The Fish would know, if anyone did. He was acknowledged to be an expert on extra-terrestrials. Anything to do with alien life forms. Space ships, unidentified flying objects, inter-galactic missiles.

Last year, when poor old Pudgy had disappeared, the Fish had even made the headlines in the local paper, the Uxenholme Times:

# UFO OVER
# UXENHOLME

Last night, whilst the good folk of Uxenholme lay asleep in their beds, an alien spaceship landed at the top of Bunkers Hill.

That, at any rate, is the claim made by Mr Clarence Trout, 45, maths teacher at St Bede's prep school.

'I was out taking a late night stroll,' says Mr Trout (affectionately known to his boys as Fish), 'when I saw this strange light appear in the sky. It was bright green, and quite blinding.

'After a while, I became aware that some kind of craft had landed. I couldn't make out the shape of it, but I distinctly saw a curtain of light dissolve to give access to the interior of the ship. As I watched, I beheld one figure go in, and another figure come out.

'Whether the figure that went in was human or alien, man or woman, whether it was abducted or went of its own free will, I am unable to say. I only report what I saw – and what I saw was very clear.'

The good Mr Trout can offer no explanation, but as a long-time believer in the existence of visitors from outer space he is not particularly surprised. When asked, 'Why Uxenholme?' his reply is short and to the point: 'Why not?'

All we can say is, why not, indeed! We look forward to future visitations.

That was when the rumour had started about Mr Potts having been abducted. Dr Dredge had not been pleased. Indeed, he had been heard to complain that the school had been made a laughing stock. The Fish was certainly a laughing stock, especially in the staff room.

'Poor old Trout and his little green men!'

'Dunno why we need his help,' said Joe, jealously. You only had to look at Mr Snitcher to see he wasn't human. Why bring a teacher into it?

'No, Harry's right, let's ask the Fish!' Ryan sat up. 'I just remembered – he's threatening a maths test tomorrow!'

'Ah…'

A quivering sigh ran round the dorm. Anything rather than a maths test!

'OK,' said Joe. 'We'll do it!'

# CHAPTER TWO
# ASKING ABOUT ALIENS

Mr Trout was happy: he was going to give Year 6 a maths test. Mr Trout enjoyed giving maths tests. It meant that while the boys were wrestling with problems – how many gallons of water would it take to fill a leaky tank? How many rolls of wallpaper would be needed to paper a room of a certain size? – Mr Trout could sit back and dream about UFOs.

Mr Trout spent most of his day dreaming about UFOs. Ones that he had seen, ones that other people had seen: ones that he had heard about, ones that he had read about. Unidentified flying objects were fast taking over Mr Trout's life. He *knew* they existed; why didn't anyone believe him?

Year 6 came surging into class, clattering and banging and making loud honking noises which passed for human speech. Mr Trout reflected, not for the first time, that teaching Year 6 was like teaching a horde of animals.

'Boys!' He clapped his hands. 'Settle down! Andrew Bicknell, what are you eating? Whatever it is, kindly swallow it at once. Ryan Daley, I saw what you just did!'

Ryan looked hurt. 'Me, sir? I didn't do anything, sir.'

'I distinctly saw you punch another boy!'

'It was only Bal, sir. We punch each other all the time.'

A zoo, thought Mr Trout, bitterly. He was teaching in a zoo. The sooner they got started on their maths test, the better.

'Baljit Singh,' he said, 'just because you have been punched it does not mean that you have to punch back. Sit, the pair of you. Everyone! Just be silent. Your behaviour appals me! I dread to think what a superior race of beings would make of you all. A very poor advertisement for humanity! Now, open your text books, please, at page 120. Questions 1 to – '

'Sir, sir!' Joe was windmilling with both arms.

'*Yes*?' said Mr Trout. He tried not to lose patience with the boys, but they really could be extraordinarily tiresome.

'Sir, when you talk about superior beings, sir, do you mean aliens, sir?'

'You may choose to call them aliens,' said Mr Trout. 'Personally I prefer to use the term extra-terrestrials. Now – '

'Do you really believe they exist, sir?'

'You know that I do,' said Mr Trout, simply. 'Now, if you – '

'Sir, what do you think they look like, sir?'

'They wouldn't look like us, would they, sir?'

'D'you reckon they'd have bug eyes, sir?'

'Do you reckon, sir?'

'That would very much depend,' said Mr Trout, 'on which planet they came from. What the conditions were. What sort of atmosphere.'

'But they would look different from us, sir, wouldn't they?'

'I would say that is a fair assumption. Now, if you would kindly open your b– '

'So, if they look different from us, sir, how come we don't notice them? I mean, if they're here with us, sir?'

'*Are* they here with us, sir?'

'Sir, are they?'

'Sir?'

'Well…' Mr Trout cleared his throat. Eighteen pairs of eyes fixed themselves anxiously upon him. For a moment Mr Trout seemed undecided. His hand still lingered over *Key Stage 2 Mathematics.* Then slowly, very slowly, he sank down on the edge of his desk. Year 6 breathed a sigh of happy relief.

'That,' said Mr Trout, 'is a good question. Are they actually here with us?'

Year 6 waited, expectantly.

'My own feelings,' said Mr Trout, 'for what they are worth – ' He paused, and knitted his fingers together. 'My own feelings are that we do indeed have extra-terrestrials amongst us. How many, of course, one cannot begin to speculate. But I would imagine a fair number.'

'In that case, sir – sir!' Ryan waved his hand like a flag. 'How come we don't recognise them, sir?'

Joe was quick with the answer: 'They'd use cloaking devices, wouldn't they, sir?'

'That is a distinct possibility,' agreed Mr Trout.

'Cos their technology would be way beyond ours, wouldn't it, sir?'

'It would, indeed! Way beyond.'

'What would a cloaking device look like, do you think, sir? Would it be like a little black box, kind of thing?'

'Strapped on their belt, or something?'

'It could be.' Mr Trout nodded. 'It could well be.'

'So that'd mean they could just press a button and – whoosh! Change in an instant.'

'And when they'd had enough – ' Bal rocketed up out of his desk – 'they could just press it again and go back to being monsters! Now I'm a human, now I'm a monster! Now I'm a human – '

It was all Year 6 needed. Within seconds, the entire room was on its feet, pressing buttons and turning into monsters. All the monsters honked and grunted and fell about, coarsely laughing, amongst the desks.

That, reflected Mr Trout wearily, was the trouble with boys. You tried to discuss something intelligent with them and they just grew over-excited and silly.

Mr Trout reached for his ruler and rapped, loudly.

'Enough! Be seated!'

Honking and panting, Year 6 clattered jubilantly back to their desks.

'Very well,' said Mr Trout. 'Let us get on! Kindly take out your – '

'Sir!' Harry's hand was up in the air. 'D'you reckon that's how it would work, sir? They could make themselves look just like us?'

'As to that,' said Mr Trout, 'I really could not say for certain. We have no knowledge of how these devices might function. Now if you would just – '

'Could work on batteries, sir. Have to be recharged.'

'Yeah!' Joe liked that idea. 'Then if they couldn't recharge 'em in time, bits of their real selves would start showing through. Fangs, and claws, and stuff.'

'Cos otherwise, how would you ever be able to recognise them, sir?'

'One has to face the possibility,' said Mr Trout, 'that we are *not* able to recognise them. Now, if you would j– '

'Are you saying, sir – ' Bal sounded incredulous – 'there could be loads of 'em just walking around all over the place and nobody knowing?'

'Why not?' said Mr Trout. He smiled and laced his fingers together. That would give them something to think about!

'I dunno.' Joe sounded doubtful. 'I reckon sooner or later they'd give themselves away.

People always do.'

'Yeah,' cried Ryan, ''cept these ain't people!'

'*Aren't* people,' said Mr Trout.

''s what I'm saying, sir. They ain't human!'

Mr Trout raised his eyes heavenwards.

'Sir!' Bal's hand was back up. 'What d'you think they're doing here, sir? D'you reckon they want to take over, sir?'

'World domination!' shouted Joe.

'D'you reckon, sir?'

Mr Trout hesitated. He seemed to be fighting some kind of inner battle.

'That's mostly what they'd come for, isn't it, sir? If their own world starts dying, and they need to find somewhere else. Kind of checking the place out, see if it's suitable.'

Weakly, Mr Trout said, 'That is one theory.'

'Are there others, sir?'

Mr Trout waved a hand.

'Don't see how they can be up to any good,' said Joe. 'Not invading someone else's world.'

That was the point at which Mr Trout lost his battle.

'Well, now,' he said. He took off his spectacles and polished them and put them back on. 'This is where it becomes interesting. Let us suppose, just for a moment, that these superior beings – for superior they undoubtedly are – have come here purely and simply as visitors. Tourists, if you will. Meaning us no harm. No evil intent. Simply here to see the sights.'

'You mean, like, on holiday, sir?'

'Precisely! Much as we would jump on a plane and fly to America, they jump on a spaceship and fly to earth.'

Mr Trout sat back in triumph. This was one of his pet theories.

There was a silence; then Bal said, 'Is that very likely, sir?'

'I see no reason why not. Imagine,' said Mr Trout, vigorously polishing his spectacles again, 'they could even have special tours. Journey to Planet Earth! See a primitive species in their natural environment! Live amongst the natives, study their ways! Some,' said Mr Trout, getting a bit carried away, 'might even choose to settle here.'

'Sir!' Bal's hand was up yet again, quivering in the air. 'When you say *here*, sir... they might even settle in this actual school, sir?'

'Might be some here right now, sir!'

'Do you think there could be, sir?'

'Here at St Bede's?' Mr Trout stroked his chin. It was an idea he had often toyed with. Certain members of staff... but no! He would not allow himself to be led up that path. Not with Year 6. They were far too easily inflamed.

'Let us not enter the realms of science fiction,' he said. 'Let us instead open our b– '

'Sir, sir!' Bal was almost falling off his chair. 'You know Mr Potts, sir?'

'Mr Potts?' What had Mr Potts to do with anything?

'D'you reckon he was the one you saw, sir? Getting into the spaceship, sir?'

'D'you think he was being abducted, sir?'

'You don't think, sir, that maybe he was just going off on holiday, sir?'

'With the aliens, sir?'

'With his luggage, sir?'

'Did he have any luggage, sir?'

'Sir, sir, when the aliens come, do they bring luggage with them, sir?'

Mr Trout's face was growing slowly purple. He was beginning to have the uncomfortable feeling that he had been manipulated. And by Year 6, of all people!

'Enough!' He peeled himself away from his desk. 'No more delay! Open your books and get to work.'

'But, sir, sir – '

'I said OPEN YOUR BOOKS!' thundered Mr Trout.

'But, sir,' cried Ryan, 'that was the bell, sir!'

Mr Trout breathed, very deeply. His chest heaved.

'Do not think you have escaped!' He forced the words out through clenched teeth. 'You have merely postponed the inevitable. The maths test,' said Mr Trout, 'will take place tomorrow.'

'Sir!' Bal waved his hand. 'We can't tomorrow, sir!'

'And why not, pray?'

'You promised we were going to do fractions, sir.'

'Fractions!' A joyous clattering and hooting broke out. Earnestly, Bal said, 'Wouldn't want to miss fractions, sir.'

'Fractions,' hissed Mr Trout, 'will have to wait.'

'But, sir, you *promised*, sir!'

Eighteen pairs of eyes stared, accusingly.

'You gave us your word, sir!'

Mr Trout sighed. He knew when he was beaten.

'Ah, Miss Beam!' He held open the door. 'Do come in.'

Miss Beam walked smiling into the room. Beautiful Miss Beam! She wasn't soft and squishy, like Mrs Jellaby. Miss Beam was perfection. She wore crisp white

shirts with stand-up collars, and smart black trousers, very tight. Her hair was dark and curly, her eyes large and brown, and her teeth as gleamingly, dazzlingly white as an advertisement for toothpaste.

The whole school was in love with Miss Beam. She taught English and had come as a replacement for Mr Potts. People naturally felt sorry for poor old Pudgy, having his nervous breakdown (or being abducted by aliens). On the whole, he had been quite popular. As Joe said, Pudgy was one of the good guys. But Miss Beam – beautiful Miss Beam! – was everybody's favourite.

Brightly, she greeted them. 'Good morning, Year 6!'

'Good morning, Miss Beam.' Year 6 chanted it politely in chorus. They didn't honk or clatter. Not with Miss Beam.

'You look as if you've been enjoying yourselves! I believe you were due to have a maths test?'

'Didn't have it, miss.' Joe announced it, proudly. 'Talked about UFOs, instead.'

'Did you, indeed?' said Miss Beam.

'All about aliens, miss, and how they come here for their holidays.'

Miss Beam raised an eyebrow.

'Some of 'em, miss, actually stay here.'

'Really?' said Miss Beam.

'Maybe in this very school, miss.'

Miss Beam gave a tinkling laugh. 'You mean, I could be sitting next to one without even realising?'

'That's it,' said Harry. 'You just wouldn't know.'

'You wouldn't, would you?' Miss Beam seemed secretly amused.

'Have to keep your eyes peeled,' said Joe. 'Watch for the signs.'

'Absolutely!' said Miss Beam. 'Watch for the signs. Who knows what you might see?'

'Fangs, miss!'

'Fangs, certainly,' agreed Miss Beam. 'Webbed feet as well, I shouldn't be surprised. Not to mention ears like satellite dishes.'

'Yeah!' Joe punched the air.

'In the meantime, however – ' Miss Beam gave one of her sweetest smiles. 'Let us take out our literacy papers and get started. Shall we?'

She didn't need to ask twice. Beautiful Miss Beam had a way with her. Nobody ever misbehaved in one of her classes.

As they filed out at the end of the lesson, Harry, in hopeful tones, said, 'You do believe in UFOs, don't you, miss?'

'Of course I do,' said Miss Beam, kindly. 'You just keep your eyes peeled – and watch out for those fangs!'

# CHAPTER THREE

# RED EYE

'Well, anyway,' said Harry, when they were in the dorm that night, after lights out, 'Miss Beam believes in UFOs. I asked her. I said, "You do believe in UFOs, don't you, miss?" and she said yes, of course she did. She wasn't being funny,' Harry assured them. 'She was serious!'

They lay there, thinking about it. The Fish was just a joke. Even the staff laughed at poor old Fish. But Miss Beam…

'She said to keep our eyes peeled,' said Harry.

'Keep a look out.' Joe agreed. 'Start with the Snitch. He's the one to watch.'

Mr Snitcher was their house master. Strange to think that only two doors away, along the corridor, an alien being could be lying in bed, hatching his alien plots.

Harry snuggled down, beneath the duvet. He heard Ryan thumping his pillow, and Joe scrabbling about in his bedside locker.

It had seemed strange, when he had first arrived, sleeping in a room with other boys. He had never wanted to come to boarding school, but with his mum and dad abroad for so much of the time it had either been that or living with his gran and granddad, who believed – or at any rate, his gran did – in Early Bedtime and Church on Sunday, not to mention Good Table Manners and Only-One-Hour-of-Television-a-Night-and-Certainly-Not-in-Your-Bedroom. As it turned out, the Head shared those beliefs, but at least Harry didn't have to suffer alone.

On the whole, boarding school wasn't so bad. He'd been hoping for midnight feasts of sardines and chocolate cake, like he'd read about, but it seemed that sardines and chocolate cake only happened in books. Joe had once smuggled a tin of condensed milk back with him after the half-term break, but he'd forgotten to bring a tin opener so Bal had had to climb out of the window and find a sharp piece of stone, which they'd spent ages bashing into the tin with a cricket bat. They'd finally managed to make a hole, and happily glugged condensed milk into their mouths and over their chins and on to their pyjamas. Unfortunately, the hole had been jagged and they'd all ended up with torn lips and had to go to Matron to have tetanus jabs.

It was probably, thought Harry, going to be more fun hunting for aliens.

He pulled the duvet up round his ears. It was only a game, of course; they didn't really believe in UFOs and space ships and all that stuff. They weren't nutters like the poor old Fish.

'Hey!' Ryan's voice suddenly honked in the darkness. 'D'you reckon he uncloaks every night?'

'Who?' Harry snaked his way eagerly back out of the duvet. 'The Snitch?'

'Yeah! Like maybe if he tried staying human too long he'd start to break down, kind of thing?'

'That's how you'd catch 'em,' said Joe. 'When bits of their real selves start showing through.'

'Whoosh!' Bal flailed excitedly. 'Now I'm human, now I'm a monster! Now I'm – ow!'

There was a loud thud, followed by a thump, followed by a strangulated cry, as Bal overbalanced and bounced off his locker on to the floor.

Almost immediately, footsteps could be heard, thudding down the passage. The door flew open. Just for a second, before the light was switched on, a pair of what looked to be red golf balls hovered in the air.

'What,' demanded Mr Snitcher, in a high-pitched screech, 'is going on?'

Four pairs of eyes blinked nervously in the light. The golf balls quivered. Bright red!

'Baljit Singh,' screeched Mr Snitcher, 'what are you doing on the floor?'

Bal scrambled hastily to his feet. 'Fell out of bed, sir.'

'Then fall back in and make sure you stay there!'

The golf balls disappeared, along with Mr Snitcher. The door slammed shut. There was a long silence, broken at last by Joe.

'Did the Snitch always have red eyes?'

'Don't think so,' said Harry.

Certainly not ones that glowed in the dark…

★ ★ ★

As well as being house master, Mr Snitcher was also Head of Year 6. This meant he had to eat breakfast with them. It was not an experience he enjoyed. Watching Year 6 eat was like watching a feeding frenzy. There was no escaping the snapping of jaws, the chomping of mouths, the spraying of crumbs. For the most part, Mr Snitcher kept his head well down over his modest bowl of sunflower seeds, which was all he ever ate. Unfortunately, it wasn't possible to blot out the noise as boys slurped on their porridge and chewed on their toast.

Harry and Joe slurped as noisily as anyone. Ryan and Bal chobbled and chewed. From time to time a foot would kick out beneath the table and a head urgently nod in Mr Snitcher's direction. If the Snitch would just look up now and again! But Mr Snitcher bent determinedly over his bowl, picking up sunflower seeds one by one and nibbling on them like a rabbit.

In the end, Joe could stand it no longer.

'Sir?' he said. 'Sir?'

'What, what? What is it?'

Mr Snitcher's head jerked up. Had one of the wretched boys managed to choke himself or set the place on fire?

The wretched boys stared, their mouths hanging open.

*The eyes which had glowed red in the night were now a dull sludge brown.*

'Well?' said Mr Snitcher.

Joe said, 'Erm…'

He looked round, rather desperately, at the others. But Harry was sitting frozen, a spoonful of porridge suspended in mid air, while marmalade dribbled and dripped off Ryan's knife and Bal, never usually at a loss for words, seemed suddenly to have been struck dumb.

'Speak, boy!' said Mr Snitcher.

'Yes, sir.' Joe gulped. 'Sorry, sir. Slip of the tongue, sir.'

Mr Snitcher placed a single sunflower seed in his mouth and stared wonderingly at Joe out of his sludge-coloured eyes. Was it his imagination, or was there something not quite right about some of these boys?

'Sorry, sir. Didn't mean to disturb you.'

'Hm,' said Mr Snitcher. Definitely something not right.

'The plot thickens,' hissed Bal, as they left the hall.

★ ★ ★

First class that day was English with Miss Beam. Beautiful Miss Beam!

'I thought this morning,' said Miss Beam, 'we would write short essays on the subject of *What I think I know about Unidentified Flying Objects*, since it seems to be something which is of great interest to you.'

*Yesss*! Year 6 liked that idea. They snatched up their pens and set to.

Harry scribbled furiously. Miss Beam's last suggestion for an essay had been *What I did over the Holiday*. Harry had spent his holiday with Gran and Granddad and had done almost nothing at all. He had managed to squeeze out just half a page in extra BIG handwriting. This was more like!

He was pleased, at the end of class, when Miss Beam picked him to read his essay out loud.

'You were the one who asked me if I believed in UFOs, so you be the one to convince me! Pretend,' said Miss Beam, 'that I am not a believer. Let us hear how persuasive you are.'

Harry cleared his throat.

*What I think I know about*
*Unidentified Flying Objects*
*(otherwise known as UFOs)*

1. I know for A FACT that they exist. This is because lots of people have seen them and sometimes have even taken photographs, which the government says are just secret spy planes and the like, but they only say this so as not to frighten the popless.

(Harry wasn't quite sure about this word. Later, in red ink, Miss Beam wrote, 'Populace. Excellent vocabulary!')

2. Because of what people report we know probably for a fact that UFOs are spaceships coming from other planets. What we don't know are which planets.

3. Also from what people report we know that these spaceships contain alien beings, also known as extra-terrestrials, meaning they

come from outside Earth. That is to say, other planets.

4. What we do not know is what these alien beings look like in their natural state as nobody as far as I am aware has ever seen them in their natural state.

5. It is a distinct possibility that they use some kind of cloaking device to make themselves resemble human beings. These would be necessary if they are going to land on Earth and mingle with us. We know for A FACT that they do land on Earth as people have seen this happen.

6. It is not so far known why they come here but there are two theeries.

('Theories,' wrote Miss Beam.)
One theery is that they want to take over, if their own world is dying, for instance, or they are

after world domination. The other theery is that they simply come here as tourists to see the sights and watch the primitive people on Earth.

7. It is known that we must be primitive compared to them as they are able to travel through space and we are not, or at least not as far. Just because they are superior, however, it does not mean they have to be hostyle.

('Hostile,' wrote Miss Beam. 'A very good point!')

8. Something else which is not known, or if it is, it is not known to me, is how they come to speak our language. It is possible, with the advanced technology they have, they can tune in to our radio and TV programmes and learn the language before they come here. Or maybe, being so superior,

their brains are able to pick it up immediately they get here. I am not sure about this.

9. Something else I wonder about, and that is food. Would our food be suitable for an alien fizeek?

('Physique,' wrote Miss Beam. 'Good thinking!')

10. To conclude, all that I have written is what I think I know about UFOs except what I said at the beginning. I know for A FACT that they exist. It is not reasonable to suppose that so many people, all over the world, would have reported seeing them if they had not, no matter what the Government says.

'Bravo!' Miss Beam clapped her hands. 'Excellent work, Harry! That would certainly be enough to convince me. I do just have to take you up on one small point

… this question of language. Surely if these beings are so superior they would have universal translators?'

'Oh! Yeah.' Harry's face lit up. 'I never thought of that!'

'You mean,' said Joe, 'they'd speak in their own language but it'd come out in human language, kind of thing?'

'And when we spoke in our language, it'd automatically be translated for them?'

'Well, that is what I would think,' agreed Miss Beam.

Bal wrinkled his brow. 'How would they do it, miss?'

Miss Beam laughed. 'That's something you would have to ask them!'

Joe said, 'I would, if I could find one.'

'Ah, well, that's the difficulty, isn't it? Finding one, when they look just the same as everyone else! Ryan, would you collect all the essays for me? Yes, Harry! Did you want to ask something?'

'What d'you think about the food, miss? D'you reckon they could eat our stuff?'

'I'm sure some of them,' said Miss Beam, 'would have no difficulty tucking into a big bowl of chips!'

Year 6 appreciated this. They honked happily. Miss Beam was known to be very fond of her chips.

'There might even be those from some planets,' she said, 'who would consider chips a rare delicacy.'

'Like when people go to France and eat snails,' suggested Ryan.

'Well, yes, maybe.' Miss Beam didn't sound quite so sure about snails. 'For my part, I think I'll stick to chips!'

'Me, too,' said Ryan. 'I'd eat chips all the time if they'd let us. Which they don't. Unfortunately.'

'Ah, well, you're not an alien!' said Miss Beam, collecting up her books. 'Well done again on that essay, Harry!'

'Know what?' said Bal, as Miss Beam left the room. 'I bet same as they can change what they look like, they can change how their bodies work. That way,' said Bal, 'they could eat whatever they like… chips, and snails, whatever turns 'em on.'

Or, said Harry, it could be that the only sort of aliens that came here were the sort that could naturally eat chips and stuff.

Joe shook his head. Far more likely, he said, they would just bring a load of pills with them.

'But we've seen them eating,' said Bal. 'All of 'em!'

At this, Joe abruptly lost interest in what aliens might eat. He gave it as his opinion that what aliens ate, or did not eat, was of very little importance. What he wanted to know was what kind of language they spoke.

'Guess that would depend,' said Ryan. 'There's got to be all different sorts out there. Could be like giant reptiles, some of 'em.'

'Or insects,' said Bal. 'I reckon if they were insects they'd most likely make clicking noises.'

'Could be all soft and jellified, like great pools of gunge, sliming about... dunno what sort of sound *they'd* make.'

'They'd plonk and gurgle,' said Joe. 'Like when your stomach's empty and it goes *blurp*.'

Five seconds later Mr Trout entered the room to find the whole of Year 6 busily blurping and plonking, clicking and gurgling, shrieking and howling. A zoo! A veritable zoo!

'What is going on?' bawled Mr Trout. 'Be quiet this instant, we are going to do fractions!'

'Oh, sir, not fractions, sir!'

'There's something we wanted to ask – '

'Being as you're an expert, sir – '

'What kind of language, sir, would aliens speak?'

Mr Trout breathed very deeply through hairy nostrils. Did the boys take him for an idiot?

'*Fractions*,' said Mr Trout.

Nobody played the same trick on him twice!

It was an interesting point, though. What kind of language *would* aliens speak?

# CHAPTER FOUR

## BLOP

Late in the night – maybe as late as midnight, but certainly long after lights out – Harry padded down the passage to the boys' bathroom. Mr Snitcher, next door, had his own bathroom. All the housemasters had. It didn't really seem quite fair, but then as Joe pointed out, life wasn't.

'No use expecting it.'

Unlike Joe, Harry couldn't honestly have said that he was bothered one way or the other. There wasn't very much that bothered Harry. He was quite a laid back sort of person. He had admittedly felt a few prickles when he'd seen the bright red golf balls floating in the dark, but maybe, after all, that had just been a trick of the light?

He left the bathroom and padded back up the passage. Yes! A trick of the light, that's all it had been. Nothing to get spooked about.

It was as he was passing Mr Snitcher's room that he heard it: a strange unearthly sound coming from somewhere inside. A kind of glooping, followed by a glurping. Could it be Mr Snitcher?

Harry crept in close and pressed his ear to the door crack. The strange sounds continued.

'*Glaaaaa-AAAAA-ergh-aaa-blurgh!*'

A pause. And then again, more vehemently this time:

'*Glaaaaa-AAAAA-ergh-aaa-BLURGH!*'

This was followed by a gloop, followed by a glurp, followed by a long-drawn-out '*Flerrrrrrgh-BLOP!*'

And then quite, quite suddenly, the door was flung open and Harry had the fright of his life. With a stifled yelp, he took to his heels and ran.

★ ★ ★

'Tell us again,' said Joe. '*What* did it sound like?'

'Like – ' Harry concentrated, trying to remember. He'd been through it all once, in the dorm before breakfast. 'Something like… glaaaa-AAAA – '

'AAAA – '

'Ergh–blaaa – '

'Ergh–blaaa –'

'Blergh – '

'Blergh – '

'Blop.'

'*Blop?*'

'Right at the end. Blop.'

'Blop. And then he opened the door – '

'Then he opened the door and he was all mad and foaming.'

'At the mouth?' Joe liked to be sure he had things right. 'Foaming at the mouth?'

'Yes, it was all frothing out of him.' Harry wriggled his fingers in front of his face. 'Great crowds of it.'

'Crowds of it.' Joe lingered lovingly over the picture of Mr Snitcher with crowds of froth coming out of his mouth. 'What about his eyes? Were they red again?'

Harry hesitated. 'Not really sure. Might have been.'

He was ashamed to admit that he hadn't hung around long enough to notice. He'd fled, in a panic, back down the corridor and hurled himself under his duvet as fast as he could, expecting the Snitch to come foaming in at any moment.

'It's all right,' said Joe. 'It was probably pretty scary. Anyway, we've already seen the eyes. Now we've heard the language... glaaa-AAAA-blergh... prob'ly communicating with a ship. Could be one out there right now, waiting to land.'

They both peered up into the sky, in search of alien vessels. The sky remained blue and clear.

'Course, they'd land at night,' said Joe. 'That's when the Fish saw them. They wouldn't risk coming in daytime. Hey, look! Isn't that your gran and granddad?'

Two or three times a term, Harry's gran and granddad would treat him and one of his friends to a special cream tea, down in the village. Gran wouldn't let Harry eat sweet things at home, she said they rotted the teeth, but she had this touching belief that the boys of St Bede's were fed on bread and marge and gristle stew for nine months of the year and were therefore entitled to a naughty treat now and again.

It was Granddad who had put the idea into her head.

'All we ever had… bread and marge and gristle stew! Eh?'

He winked at the boys as they settled themselves into a corner at the Merrie Kettle.

'Don't suppose anything has changed much since my time?'

Earnestly, they assured him that it hadn't.

'We're pretty well always starving,' said Harry.

'Know the feeling,' said Granddad. 'You stoke up while you've got the chance!'

'Order whatever you like,' smiled Gran.

Joe and Harry studied the menu. There were meringues with fresh cream; doughnuts with jam; fairy cakes with sprinkles; chocolate cake with butter icing; and fruit cake with fruit. Joe and Harry ordered two of everything except the fruit cake.

'Why not go for the lot?' said Granddad. 'What's wrong with the poor old fruit cake?'

'No icing,' said Harry.

'Ah.' Granddad pulled a face. 'How stupid of me!'

Gran settled back cosily into her seat. 'So what's been happening at school?'

Gran always wanted to know what had been happening at school. Harry racked his brains for something to tell her.

'We think one of the teachers might be an alien,' he said.

'If not several,' added Joe.

Granddad nodded, wisely. 'Shouldn't be surprised,' he said.

'Oh, Arthur, really!' said Gran.

'No, it's true,' insisted Joe. 'We know for a fact about one of 'em.'

Granddad chuckled. 'Saw him land, did you?'

'Harry heard him talk.' Joe turned excitedly to Harry. 'Tell them what it sounded like!'

'Glaaa–AAAA–blergh,' warbled Harry obligingly.

A lady at the next table looked at him in some surprise.

'Harry, hush!' said Gran.

'I was just demonstrating,' said Harry.

'I'm sure you were, dear, but not in public. It's vulgar. It sounds to me as if the poor man was having a choking fit.'

'Sounds to me like some kind of alien tongue,' said Granddad.

Gran tutted impatiently.

'We reckon he was using his communicator,' said Joe.

'*Yes!*' Granddad banged his fist triumphantly on the table.

Gran said, 'Arthur, please.'

'Sorry, m'dear.' Granddad put a finger to his lips. 'Not in public!'

'Thing is,' said Joe, 'we reckon there could be a whole nest of 'em.'

'Nothing new,' said Granddad, 'nothing new! Always been aliens at St Bede's. Plenty of 'em in my day, I can tell you.'

Gran said, 'Arthur, don't tease.'

'Me, tease?' Granddad rolled his eyes. 'True as I sit here! Place was riddled with 'em. One chap, I remember, old Gorraby – ' Granddad gave another of his throaty chuckles. 'Didn't even look human!'

'This is it.' Joe leaned forward, eagerly. 'Half of 'em don't!'

'We got one guy?' said Harry. 'He's got this eye keeps falling out?'

'Falling out?' said Gran. 'His *eye?*'

'Keeps going plop! Then he yells at people not to tread on it.'

'I should think he does!' said Gran.

'We reckon,' said Joe, 'it's got something to do with his cloaking device.'

Gran was looking bewildered. 'What, pray, is a cloaking device and what does it have to do with the poor man's eye falling out?'

'It's this thing?' said Harry. 'Thing they use to make themselves look human?'

'Yeah, and if it's not working properly,' explained Joe, 'then bits of 'em'd probably start dropping off.'

'Or even,' said Harry, 'disappearing altogether.'

Gran turned slowly to Granddad. 'Arthur,' she said, 'what are they talking about?'

'Cloaking devices, m'dear.' Granddad patted her hand. 'Don't worry about it. Here come the cakes!'

When the cakes had all been eaten, and the last few crumbs splatted up on wet fingertips, Gran said it was time to be getting them back.

'Back to prison, eh?' Granddad chuckled again. 'Back to bread and water!'

As they were leaving, they caught sight of Miss Beam, over in the far corner. She was tucking into an enormous bowl of chips.

She looked up and saw them, and waved hello.

'That's Miss Beam,' said Harry.

'She's our English teacher,' said Joe.

'Is she, by Jove?' Granddad's eyes swivelled appreciatively in Miss Beam's direction. 'Well! We certainly didn't have anyone like that in my young day.'

In warning tones, Gran said, 'Arthur!'

'Yes, m'dear.' Granddad made a trumpeting sound down his nose. 'Sorry, m'dear. A bit carried away.'

'You should be ashamed of yourself,' said Gran. 'A man of your age!'

'Everybody loves Miss Beam,' said Harry.

'Hm!'

Gran hustled Granddad out on to the pavement. 'You say she's one of your teachers? What on earth was the woman doing? Gorging herself on chips!'

'She likes chips,' said Harry. 'She reckons they're a delicacy.'

'Have to say that I agree with her,' said Granddad.

He sounded rather wistful; Granddad wasn't allowed to eat chips.

'I'm appalled,' said Gran, 'that a *teacher* should set such a bad example.'

'She's not the only one.' Harry sprang at once to Miss Beam's defence. 'We had another teacher used to like 'em, too. Mr Hodge. Used to bring bags of 'em into class.'

'That is outrageous!' said Gran. And then, rather sharply: 'Where did he get them from?'

Harry shrugged. 'Kitchen, I s'ppose.'

'Are you telling me they do *chips*?' said Gran. 'At *St Bede's*? I was led to believe you had nothing but gristle stew!'

'Yeah, we have plenty of that,' Joe assured her. 'Looks like washing-up water with bits floating in it.'

'Tastes like washing-up water, too,' said Harry.

'Gristle stew is what we have most days. Chips is just, like, occasional.'

'Hardly ever, really.'

'Can't honestly remember the last time we had 'em.'

'I'm afraid,' said Gran, 'I don't believe a word that either of you say. Or you!' She gave Granddad a prod.

Granddad started, and said, 'Yes, m'dear! Absolutely!'

Slowly, because of Gran's knees, they made their way back up the High Street and round the side of the hill to St Bede's.

'We reckon,' said Joe, waving a hand, 'up there is where they land their ships.'

'Ships?' said Gran. 'What ships? How could ships land on a hill?'

Very solemnly Granddad said, 'The lad is talking about spaceships, Martha.'

'Oh, we're starting that again, are we?' said Gran. 'Such nonsense, all of it! I do wish you wouldn't encourage them.'

'Won't do them any harm,' said Granddad. 'Never did me any, and goodness knows, I've been taught by a few aliens in my time!'

As they neared the school gates a strange, knobbly figure appeared, dressed in bright red Lycra. It was Mr Snitcher, doing his jogging. He ran with his knees up in the air and his feet splayed out.

'That's him,' hissed Harry. 'The one we were telling you about.'

'The poor man with the eye?' said Gran.

'No,' said Harry, 'the other one.'

'The alien?' Granddad turned to watch as Mr Snitcher went jogging off through the gates. 'Ye-e-e-s. I see what you mean!'

'Hey!' Joe had hung back. They turned, to let him catch up. 'Did you notice that thing on his wrist?' said Joe. 'That little black box thing? You don't think – ' He looked first at Harry, then at Granddad.

'You don't think it could have been a cloaking device, do you?'

'Absolutely!' said Granddad. 'I should say that's exactly what it was.'

'Oh, Arthur, for heaven's sake,' cried Gran, 'don't be so silly!'

# CHAPTER FIVE

## NOT A NORMAL HUMAN

Joe and Harry could hardly wait to get back and give the others their news.

'Man!' cried Ryan, when he heard. 'That is awesome!'

'Awesome,' agreed Bal. He chortled. 'The plot thickens!'

'Reckon it's all the proof we need. Couldn't hardly believe it,' said Joe. 'Little black box thing, strapped on his wrist!'

'Right out in the open,' marvelled Harry. 'You'd have thought at least he'd keep it somewhere people couldn't see.'

'Shows he doesn't care,' said Joe. 'Just cos we're not as advanced as his lot, he prob'ly thinks we don't know about UFOs and stuff.'

'Yeah.' Ryan nodded. 'Like we're so dumb we can't recognise a cloaking device when we see one.'

There was a pause.

'I suppose it *was* a cloaking device?' said Bal.

Joe looked at him in some annoyance. 'What else could it be?'

'I dunno! A watch, maybe?'

'Wasn't a watch,' said Harry.

'Compass? In case he gets lost?'

'How could he get lost, just running down the road?'

'Could if he didn't have any sense of direction. Like if aliens don't understand left and right same as we do.'

'There was that one time,' said Ryan, doubtfully, 'when he told us the right hand didn't know what the left hand was doing. I mean, what's that about? You'd have to be pretty stupid, not knowing what your hands were doing.'

'Not if you were an alien,' said Bal. 'Just means you're built different. Like maybe on his home planet he goes by smell, or something. Vibrations. Like an insect, sort of thing. So then he comes to Earth and he gets all confused. Has to have a compass. That's all I'm saying.'

'Yeah, well, you weren't there,' said Joe. 'You didn't see it. We did. Anyway, Harry's granddad reckoned it was a cloaking device. Didn't he?'

'He did,' said Harry.

It was true that Gran had told him not to be so silly, but what did Gran know? She'd probably gone to an all-girls' school where they didn't have aliens. Or if they did, she wouldn't have recognised them. He wasn't being sexist! Miss Beam didn't like it when they were sexist. He just reckoned Granddad knew a bit more about aliens than Gran.

''cording to Harry's granddad,' said Joe, 'there's always been aliens on the staff. Didn't even look human, half of 'em.

That's what he said. What was the name of that one? Gottleby, or something?'

'Gorraby,' said Harry. 'Mr Gorraby.'

'What kind of name is that?' said Bal.

'Kind of name,' said Joe, 'that'd appeal to an alien. Same like Snitcher. I bet what they do, I bet they Google on their computers for lists of human names, then pick out the ones they like. Stands to reason they'd like different ones from us.'

'Why?' said Bal.

'Cos they're aliens!'

Bal said, 'Mm. Maybe.'

'Dunno why you always have to *argue*,' said Joe. And then, very quickly, before Bal could start up again, 'Know what we ought to do? See if we can find this Gorraby guy in a school photo. See what he looked like.'

Even Bal was prepared to admit that this was a good idea. In the main corridor at St Bede's there were photographs of boys and teachers going back almost eighty years.

'How old's your granddad?' said Joe. 'When d'you reckon he was here?'

Harry wasn't sure. He thought about …
fifty years ago? Maybe more.

'*More?*' said Ryan.

'He's pretty ancient,' said Harry.

'Let's go and see if we can find him,' said
Joe. 'I want to see this Gorraby guy!'

They discovered Harry's granddad,
sitting cross-legged in the front row of a
photograph that had been taken fifty-three
years previously. Fifty-three years! They
gazed upon it, in awe.

'To think he's still walking around,' said
Ryan.

'They do,' said Joe. 'Hey, look! I reckon
that's Mr Gorraby, that one there.'

The others crowded round to look
where Joe's finger was pointing.

A large man with a face like a potato
stared back at them.

'Reckon that's him,' said Joe.

'Could be this one.' Bal pointed excitedly
at another candidate: a sad, droopy man with
eyes half way down his face and ear lobes so
long they almost reached his shoulders.

'How about this?' squeaked Ryan.

'Or this?' said Harry.

Aliens stared out from all over. There were noses like door knockers, eyes like satellite dishes. Teeth that stuck out, mouths that sucked in. Necks like flagpoles, or no necks at all. Heads the size of peanuts, heads sunk into shoulders.

'Blimey,' said Joe. 'I reckon your granddad was right!'

Harry slowly nodded. 'I reckon.'

It was true that as well as telling Granddad not to be silly, Gran had also told him not to tease. Granddad did enjoy pulling Harry's leg occasionally, like the time he had asked him if he would care for some dates and when Harry had said yes, please, Granddad told him, "Go and take some off the calendar, then!" and roared with laughter at his own wit. You couldn't always trust Granddad to be quite serious.

Still, it was strange how these rumours had come down over the years. You didn't have rumours for no reason.

'Tell you what,' said Harry. 'Let's make a list!'

Joe, immediately, said, 'List of what?'

'Facts,' said Harry. 'Stuff we know.'

Joe, just a tiny bit resentful, pointed out that he had already done a list for Miss Beam. What was the point of doing it all over again?

They wouldn't be doing it all over again, said Harry. Miss Beam's list had been about UFOs. His list would be about Mr Snitcher.

'Known Facts,' said Harry. 'So's we can work out where we're at.'

The trouble with Harry, he had a brain like a filing cabinet. He liked everything to be neatly labelled and sorted. Joe's brain was more like a fizzy water fountain with ping pong balls bouncing up and down. Joe was an action man. He didn't see the need for lists. But Harry wanted to make one, and Harry was his friend, and Harry's gran and granddad had, after all, treated them to a really good tea.

'Yeah, OK,' said Joe. 'We can do one, if that's what you want.'

This was Harry's list:

### KNOWN FACTS ABOUT MR SNITCHER

Fact no.1: He does not look like a real human being

Fact no.2: He speaks an alien language

Fact no.3: His eyes go red in the dark

Fact no.4: He foams at the mouth

Fact no.5: He wears a cloaking device.

'I reckon that just about wraps it up,' said Harry. 'I reckon that's proof enough for anyone.'

Even Bal didn't argue. The question was, what did they do next?

What they did next, said Joe, was stay on the case. There were bound to be more clues if they just kept their eyes peeled.

'Bound to be stuff we've missed… could be just lying there, right under our noses.'

Stuff was indeed just lying there, under their noses. It was Joe himself who drew attention to it.

'Ever noticed,' he said, 'how he eats the same thing for breakfast every morning?'

'Yeah.' They nodded. 'Sunflower seeds.'

'I put it to you,' said Joe. 'That's normal?'

Now that he mentioned it, they all agreed that it obviously wasn't.

'Might be normal for parrots,' said Bal.

'Might be normal for aliens,' said Joe. 'Who knows what sort of stuff they like to eat?'

'That's exactly what I said in my essay.'

Harry couldn't resist reminding him of it. 'What kind of food do they eat? You said it wasn't important.'

'Yeah, well, it's not, *as such*,' said Joe. 'Can't prove someone's an alien just cos they eat sunflower seeds.'

'He never eats proper lunches, either,' said Ryan. 'I've seen him. Like the other day, when we had fish and chips? He was sat there, with a bunch of lettuce leaves? Next to Miss Beam, he was.'

Beautiful Miss Beam! They all sighed. What bliss to sit next to Miss Beam!

'She was eating her chips,' said Ryan, 'while he was munching on lettuce. Instead of chips!'

'Yeah, he doesn't eat chocolate pudding, either,' said Harry.

He took out his list. 'That's another fact.' He added it, as no.6.

*Fact no.6: Doesn't eat chocolate pudding or chips.*

'This is weird,' said Bal. Chocolate pudding and chips were the closest they ever came to proper food.

'Obviously something we're going to have to investigate,' said Joe.

It was Bal, at breakfast next morning, who dared to ask the question.

'Sir, do you like sunflower seeds, sir?'

Mr Snitcher raised mournful eyes from his plate. 'You think I eat these things for pleasure?'

'You mean, you don't enjoy them, sir?'

'Would you?' said Mr Snitcher.

'I don't think I would, sir.'

'Well, there you go.' Mr Snitcher popped a seed into his mouth and chewed, glumly.

'Sir!' Joe leaned forward. 'If you don't like them, sir, why don't you eat a normal breakfast same as everyone else, sir?'

Mr Snitcher said, 'Huh!' And then, with an air of morbid satisfaction, 'That is because I am not the same as everyone else.'

Excuse me??? Harry choked on his porridge. Mr Snitcher was *admitting* it?

'I am cursed,' said Mr Snitcher, 'with allergies. *Multiple* allergies. Allergies without number! There is practically nothing,' said Mr Snitcher, proudly, 'that I am able to consume without putting my life in danger. If I were to swallow but *one peanut*, my face would blow up like a beach ball and I should die. If I were to eat the merest *sliver* of cheese, my tongue would swell in my mouth and suffocate me. As for wheat – ' Mr Snitcher gave an elaborate shudder. 'Do not speak to me of wheat! Just one grain and I should be immediately and violently ill. I am not,' said Mr Snitcher, with a sad, suffering smile, 'a normal human being.'

He was! He was actually admitting it!

As Bal said later, 'The plot grows even thicker...'

# CHAPTER SIX

## CLOSE ENCOUNTER

Harry couldn't sleep. He heard the church clock, down in the village, striking midnight, and still he tossed and turned and thumped at his pillow.

Something was bothering him. Something they had talked about with Gran and Granddad. He had this feeling there was a question that needed to be asked, but the more he tried to think what it could be, the more his brain tied itself into knots until he felt that the inside of his head was buzzing with a swarm of bees.

Maybe he should go to the bathroom. He didn't need to go to the bathroom, but just getting out of bed and walking down the corridor might help.

He threw back the duvet – and then stopped. Maybe going to the bathroom wouldn't be such a good idea after all. Not with mad aliens on the loose, foaming at the mouth. For all he knew, the Snitch might spend the entire night with his ear to the door crack, waiting to leap out on unsuspecting boys.

The trouble was, now he had thought about going to the bathroom he suddenly desperately needed to. If he hadn't thought about it, he'd have been all right.

His legs were starting to twitch. He stuck one out of the bed and wriggled his toes. Then he stuck the other out the other side. Then he humpled over, on to his front, both arms under the pillow. The pillow was full of lumps and bumps. Harry flung himself about the bed, trying to get comfortable. The church clock chimed the quarter.

It was no use, he would have to go! Slowly and reluctantly, Harry eased himself out from under the duvet. For a minute he was tempted to wake Joe, just for a bit of company, but that would be too much like being four years old all over again. When Harry had been four years old he had been scared to go upstairs by himself at Gran and Granddad's because of the monster that lived in the attic. He was eleven now! You didn't ask your best friend to go to the bathroom with you when you were eleven years old, not even if there were a whole horde of mad aliens foaming at the mouth, waiting to spring out at you.

Harry took a deep breath, slipped through the door and did a record-breaking dash along the corridor. He had never moved so fast in all his life! Mr O'Hooligan would have been proud of him.

As he sprinted, there and back, he caught snatches of alien language.

'*Glaaaaaa-AAAAA-ergh...*'

The Snitch was at it again! Using his communicator. Perhaps they got cheap rates if they called after midnight? Or maybe that was the best time for getting through? Atmospherics, or something.

Harry took a flying leap back into bed and pulled the duvet up. His heart was pounding, but at least his head wasn't full of bees any more. He knew, now, what it was that had been nagging at him.

He was about to give Joe a prod, in the next bed, when he heard the sound of a door opening. Mr Snitcher! Harry froze, expecting him at any moment to come bursting in, frothing and foaming, eyes gleaming a ferocious red in the darkness. But then there was a creaking of floor boards, and footsteps moving off, along the corridor.

Phew! Harry felt a trickle of perspiration down his spine. It was no joke, sleeping next door to an alien.

'Hey!' He leaned across and poked at Joe. 'You awake?'

'Wozz madder?' Joe mumbled grumpily.

'You know Mr Hodge?'

Joe grunted.

'I was just thinking,' said Harry. 'I can remember him bringing bags of chips into class, cos it was like my first term and I'd never known a teacher do that before. I thought it was pretty cool! Remember how he used to chuck 'em at us if we weren't paying attention?'

'Yeah.' Joe propped himself on an elbow. He remembered that, all right. Sometimes they hadn't paid attention on purpose, in the hope of getting a few chips lobbed in their direction. Mr Hodge had been OK!

'And then he suddenly left,' said Harry, 'and Mr Potts came, and I was just wondering, didn't Mr P– '

Joe never discovered what it was that Harry was wondering, for at that moment there came a strange sound, as of something being ripped apart, almost as if the sky itself were being torn open, while at the same time a flash of brilliant green lit up the dorm.

Joe and Harry flung themselves out of bed and across to the window.

'Wossup?'

That was Bal, blinking in the sudden brightness.

'Woss goin' on?'

That was Ryan, blearily opening his eyes.

'Look!'

Joe was pointing. They scrambled across to join him and Harry at the window.

'Wow…'

They stood, transfixed, staring out into the night. The light had faded, leaving an eerie glow, like a green mist, encircling the top of Bunker's Hill.

'What is it?' whispered Ryan.

'They've landed,' said Joe.

Dimly, they made out a large, saucer-like shape emerging from the mist.

'It's a ship…'

Even Joe sounded awestruck. He might have told Harry's granddad that Bunker's Hill was where the alien ships touched down, but he'd never expected it to actually happen. It had just been a game! Nobody really believed it was true. Like the poor

old Fish and his UFOs. Nobody *believed* him.

They crammed at the window, watching as the mist slowly cleared. The saucer-like shape seemed to skim the surface, then finally settle, just out of sight, behind a ridge of trees.

Nobody suggested that they should leave the safety of the dorm and go creeping out to investigate. Not even Joe was bold enough for that.

But then, as they watched, a figure appeared, making its way across the playing field. They saw it open the gate and set off down the path. It was heading for the hill!

Harry's fingers felt for Joe's arm and gripped it. Ryan swallowed.

'Who is it?'

'Gotta be the Snitch,' said Harry.

Joe pressed his nose to the window, trying to get a better view, but the figure was too far off.

'Gotta be,' said Harry. 'I heard him leave his room just a few seconds ago.'

Joe narrowed his eyes. It certainly looked like it could be the Snitch.

There was a pause.

'Guess we prob'ly ought to go and make sure.'

Joe said it as carelessly as he could, like it was no big deal. Just tracking an extra-terrestrial up the side of a hill at dead of night as it went to meet an alien spacecraft. Nothing to get freaked out about.

'What d'you reckon?' said Joe.

'Yeah.' Harry nodded. 'I reckon we ought.'

Wouldn't that be something to tell Granddad? Then let Gran sniff and say they were just being silly!

'You coming, then?' said Joe. He threw open the window. 'Down the fire escape!'

One by one, they clambered out. Harry couldn't decide which he was more scared of, being caught by aliens or caught by Dr Dredge. Boys had been expelled before now for climbing out of dormitory windows.

'Quick or we'll lose him!' Joe was already down on the ground and haring off in the direction of the playing field. The others raced after him.

Across the field they ran, out through the gate and down the lane.

'I can't see him,' panted Ryan.

'There he goes!'

Joe shot off again, the others in hot pursuit.

Ahead of them, a dim and distant figure in the moonless night, the Snitch strode on, making for the top of the hill.

'Hang back,' hissed Joe. 'Don't want him seeing us!'

Slowly, bent almost double, they crept from bush to bush. The sky above was cloudless, filled with a mass of twinkling stars. The Snitch, ahead of them, seemed but a thin black stick in the silver light.

They crouched, and watched, as he reached the summit and dropped down, out of sight, behind the ridge of trees.

'After him!'

With Joe leading the way, they charged forward.

'OK!' Joe flapped a hand. 'Down!'

Obediently, they dropped to the ground. Even Bal, for once, didn't argue. On hands and knees they crawled the last few yards to the top.

There, just for a moment, they hesitated. Which one of them was going to be brave enough to stick his head over the parapet?

Joe! The man of action.

He slithered forward, hugging the grass. The others held their breath.

Centimetre by cautious centimetre, Joe raised his head. His eyes widened. His jaw dropped.

'What is it?' hissed Ryan.

Joe said nothing; just went on staring. Harry could contain himself no longer. He inched forward next to Joe and peered over. Ryan and Bal scrabbled after him, until they were all four at the ridge, all four peering over.

And now four jaws were dropping, four pairs of eyes pinned wide.

Below the ridge was a shallow dip. In the dip was an object. Large, and metallic. Saucer-shaped. Still wreathed in the remnants of a green mist.

As they watched, an opening appeared in the side of the object. It was not so much a door as a curtain of light.

The Snitch marched boldly up. He was going to go in!

The light dissolved as the Snitch walked through; and for a split second, before he disappeared, they thought they saw fangs. And fur. And a thing like a beak.

And now something else was happening. They could make out a vague shape in the curtain of light. Something was coming out!

This time they did see fangs, and fur, and a thing like a beak. Except that this time it definitely was a beak...

Harry tried to swallow, but his mouth had gone dry. He felt as if he had a razor

blade stuck in his throat. Joe, next to him, seemed to have stopped breathing. Ryan and Bal were frozen like statues.

The thing stood for a moment, as if testing the atmosphere. The great beak slowly opened, revealing a gaping chasm. A tongue, like a whiplash, darted out and back again. The beak, with a loud clack, snapped itself shut. Satisfied, the thing grunted and moved forward through the curtain.

The fur which covered it was thick, and sleek, and gingery brown. What had seemed to be fangs now looked more like tusks on either side of the beak. They rose up, questing and quivering, through the thicket of fur. Eyes like twin Catherine wheels popped and pulsated, spinning in different directions.

The thing came out into the night and with purposeful steps began to stride up the side of the valley, towards the ridge of trees where the four boys were crouched.

Nobody waited for Joe to say 'Move!'

They were up on their feet and tearing back down the hill as fast as their legs would carry them.

# CHAPTER SEVEN
## IF NOT ... THEN WHO?

Back in the safety of the dorm, they slammed the window shut, flung themselves on to their beds, and broke into a frenzied babble.

Did you see the beak? Did you see the eyes? Did you see the fur? They all agreed on what they had seen: a fur-covered, bug-eyed monster, with quivering tusks and a beak like that of a giant bird.

Harry said, 'I s'ppose we're not just dreaming?'

But how could they all have the same dream? And what about the Snitch? The Snitch had gone. They had trailed him up the hill, they had watched him walk towards the ship, they had seen him disappear through the curtain of light.

He had obviously suspected something. Got wind of the fact that people were on to him. The rumour, after all, had been around for weeks. He must have called the mother ship and told them to come and pick him up before he was rumbled.

That still didn't explain the fur-covered *thing* that had landed in his place. But at least it showed they'd been right about the Snitch.

Harry had just started to say so, trying to sound a little bit triumphant and pretend that fur-covered bug-eyed monsters didn't bother him one little bit, when to everyone's alarm the door was suddenly flung open and the light snapped on. They stared, speechless, at a sticklike figure in polka dot pyjamas.

'Why,' demanded Mr Snitcher, irritably, 'am I hearing voices at one o'clock in the morning?'

There was a stunned silence. Not even Joe had an answer to give.

'Some of us,' snarled Mr Snitcher, 'are attempting to get some rest. In my state of health, I cannot afford to be deprived of my sleep. It is essential I have my full eight hours. Kindly lie yourselves down and cease this intrusive chitter chatter!'

The light was snapped off, the door closed. There was a long silence; then Harry's voice came quavering into the dark:

'If it wasn't the Snitch...'

He didn't finish the sentence; he didn't need to. They were all asking themselves the same question.

If it wasn't the Snitch who had disappeared into the spaceship, then who was it?

★ ★ ★

'Could have been any of 'em, really,' said Joe, as they crawled, bleary-eyed, out of bed the next morning. 'I reckon most of 'em's prob'ly aliens.'

Harry objected. It couldn't have been Mrs Jellybaby, they would have recognised her from her shape. Any of the others, maybe.

'And just cos it wasn't the Snitch doesn't mean he's not one of 'em,' said Ryan.

Joe agreed. It may not have been the Snitch whom they had trailed up the hill, but he obviously wasn't human.

'Not when his eyes keep going red.'

'And don't forget the cloaking device,' urged Bal. 'I reckon you're right, there's a whole nest of 'em!'

'What we ought to do,' said Joe, 'we ought to see who's missing… gotta be one of 'em!'

They set off along the passage, but before they had gone more than a few steps Mr Snitcher's door had burst open and the Snitch himself sprang out at them like a Jack-in-the-box on the end of a wire.

'Ah! The very people I am looking for. I wish you to know,' said Mr Snitcher, 'that

I have been awake, on and off, almost the entire night!'

They shuffled, nervously. Round Mr Snitcher's mouth there were traces of foam.

Harry muttered, 'Sorry about that, sir! Didn't mean to upset you, sir.'

'Whether you meant to or not is beside the point. The fact is that you did. I shall be a nervous wreck all day. I simply cannot function without my full eight hours! Now, get in here, the four of you, I need you to find something for me. Down there!'

He pointed. Bal said, 'Down there, sir?'

'On the floor! My contact lens. I dropped it whilst I was gargling.'

'G-gargling, sir?'

'Yes,' said Mr Snitcher. 'Gargling! *Glaaaaa-AAAAA-ergh*... gargling!'

He paused. Four pairs of eyes stared up at him. Four mouths dropped open.

'Do I perhaps hear you inquire − ' Mr Snitcher cupped a hand to one of his big pancake ears − 'why was I gargling at the same time as attempting to remove my contact lens? I will tell you why! It was because I was running late. And the reason I was running late? Because my sleep pattern was interrupted! So, if you would just get down there and locate my missing property, we can all proceed to breakfast. Such as it is,' said Mr Snitcher, in tones of some bitterness. 'In my case, a mere handful of seeds and a glass of water. I am a martyr to my health at the best of times. Being rudely awoken in the middle of the night does nothing for my digestive system.'

'No, sir.' Harry nodded, gravely. 'I can see that it wouldn't, sir.'

'Just get on with it,' said Mr Snitcher.

They fell to their knees and began a slow crawl across the carpet.

'Sir,' said Ryan, 'please, sir! I'm not sure I know what a contact lens looks like, sir.'

'Small,' said Mr Snitcher. 'And red. And exceedingly delicate!'

'Sir, did you say *red*, sir?' Ryan sat back on his heels. 'Wouldn't that make your eyes go a bit of a funny colour, sir?'

Mr Snitcher's top lip curled. 'What sort of a funny colour did you have in mind, precisely?'

'Well, like… red?' said Ryan.

'Red!' Mr Snitcher gave a little snicker of laughter. 'Was that a wild guess, I wonder, or did you actually employ your brain?'

Ryan looked round, rather doubtfully, at the others. 'Just wondered why anyone'd want red eyes, sir.'

'To frighten small boys?' said Mr Snitcher. 'The fact is, I have been invited – ' his chest swelled, slightly – 'to a fancy dress party being thrown by the Head Master's wife. I intend,' said Mr Snitcher, 'to go as a vampire.'

There was a silence. Then very politely Harry said, 'Wouldn't you need fangs for that, sir?'

'I have fangs,' said Mr Snitcher. A giggle burst from him. 'I made them out of orange peel!'

Bal said, 'Oh, that's brilliant, sir! I'm sure you'll make a very convincing vampire, sir.'

'Only,' said Mr Snitcher, 'if I have my contact lens!'

'Don't worry, sir.' Bal crawled hastily off across the floor. 'We'll find it for you.'

'Sir, sir! What's this, sir?'

Joe was holding out a small black box on a strap.

Greatly daring, Bal said, 'It looks like a cloaking device, sir.'

'Cloaking device? What are you babbling about? That,' said Mr Snitcher, 'is my pedometer. It measures how many steps I take when I go for my jogs. An essential tool to maintain my well-being. Kindly put it back where you found it. And you!' He poked at Ryan, busily crawling off towards the window. 'You're going in the wrong direction!'

Ryan was about to turn himself round when Bal gave a triumphant cry.

'Sir, I think I've got it, sir!'

He stabbed at something with his finger. Mr Snitcher let out a screech.

'Careful, careful, you'll damage it!'

'Are you going to go to breakfast wearing it, sir?'

'Certainly not,' said Mr Snitcher. 'The Head Master would be most displeased.'

'But don't you need to practise, sir?'

'I find it best at night.' Mr Snitcher giggled again. 'They glow, you know, in the dark!'

So that, thought Harry, was that. Red contact lenses and a pedometer. And *gargling*. Huh!

'Still doesn't mean he's not one of 'em,' said Joe, as they clattered down the stairs to the dining hall.

'I dunno.' Harry wasn't quite so sure. Obviously *somebody* on the staff had been one of them; just not the Snitch. The Snitch was obviously just a bit weird. A bit mad. Lots of teachers were.

'Anyway,' said Joe, 'we'll check 'em out in assembly. See who's missing.'

Nobody was, as far as Harry could make out. All the prime suspects were there, including Mrs Jellybaby, though for the moment she didn't really count.

There was Mr Bulstrode, spluttering enthusiastically into the ear of a reluctant Mr Trout. There was Monsieur Tittinbot, nervously fingering his glass eye. Mr O'Hooligan, a football already clamped between his beefy thighs. Mr McNutter, absent-mindedly gnawing on a pencil.

Dr Dredge, at the lectern, standing on one leg like a stork. Who was missing?

And then he realised... there *was* one person who wasn't there.

# CHAPTER EIGHT

# MR SMITH GETS HIS CHIPS

The Head Master made the announcement at the end of assembly. *With deep regret… sudden emergency… called back home… will be greatly missed.*

Right up until that moment, Harry had been secretly hoping it wasn't true. Even now, he found it hard to get his head round the idea. It just didn't seem possible!

'Reckon we ought to tell someone?' said Joe, as they left the hall.

But who could they tell?

'The Fish?' said Ryan.

'Yeah.' Joe nodded. 'Tell the Fish!'

If anyone were going to believe them, it

would be Mr Trout.

He was there, at his desk, as they filed in for their first lesson.

'Sit!' said Mr Trout. 'What are you waiting for?'

'Need to speak to you, sir.'

'About mathematics, I trust?'

'N–not exactly, sir. The fact is, sir – '

'*Yes*?' said Mr Trout. 'The fact is…?'

Joe took a deep breath and launched into the story. The others rushed to his support.

'It's a fact, sir!'

'Saw it with our own eyes, sir!'

'All of us, sir!'

'Sorry, boys.' Mr Trout shook his head. 'You may have got away with it once, you're not getting away with it again. I will not be sidetracked a second time! Be seated, we have work to do.'

'But, sir, please, sir, this is serious!'

They clustered round the desk, earnestly beseeching him to listen.

'It's true, sir! We saw it happen, sir!'

'We did, sir!'

'Top of Bunkers Hill, just like you said!'

'It was definitely a ship, sir! Could even have been the same one you saw.'

'Had this strange glow, sir – '

'Kind of greenish.'

'And this sort of opening, in the side.'

'Like a curtain.'

'Curtain of light, sir. Like in the paper.'

'And this one person that went in, and this – this *thing* that came out.'

'It was like a horror film, sir! Like a monster.'

'Had these big bug eyes – '

'And fur – '

'All covered in it!'

'All gingery!'

'And a beak, sir! It had a beak!'

Mr Trout smiled a tight little smile. 'And no doubt claws and fangs and eyes like Catherine wheels?'

'They were, sir! They were! That's exactly what they were like!'

'Your imagination,' said Mr Trout, 'knows no bounds. But I fear your efforts are wasted. I do not fall for the same trick twice.'

'But, sir!' protested Bal.

'It hurts, doesn't it,' said Mr Trout, 'when people don't believe you?'

'We believed you, sir!'

'We always believed you!'

'Really?' said Mr Trout. Plainly not convinced.

'Honestly, sir! That's why we've come to you.'

'And what, precisely, would you expect me to do?'

'Thought maybe you could... go to the newspaper, sir?'

'And tell them what? That another spaceship has landed?'

'Only this time, sir, you could say about the aliens... how one went in and one came out.'

'Cos last time, sir, you weren't sure. You didn't know they were aliens.'

'Do you take me for a fool?' said Mr Trout. 'I have already been made a laughing stock once! You wish me now to tell the world that the staff of St Bede's is infested with extra-terrestrials?'

'Only one, sir. As far as we know. And they've gone, now, sir.'

'To Australia, boy! To Australia! A family emergency. Do you doubt the Head Master's words?'

'Reckon he might have been hoodwinked, sir.'

'In that case,' said Mr Trout, 'I suggest you go and tell him yourself! In the meanwhile, just be seated along with the rest of the class and take out your books. Page 121!'

'But, sir,' bleated Harry.

'No more!' thundered Mr Trout.

Defeated, they went to their desks.

Harry took out his maths book. Mechanically, he opened it at page 121. A jumble of words and figures danced before his glazed eyes. All he could think about was Miss Beam. Beautiful Miss Beam!

Who could ever have guessed that she of all people would turn out to be an alien? Not Mr Bulstrode. Not Mrs Jellybaby. Not the McNutter, not the O'Hooligan, not the Head Master. Not even Monsieur Tittinbot, with his dodgy eye. But beautiful Miss Beam! The last person anyone would have suspected.

Or was she?

Something stirred at the back of Harry's mind. Something that had been nagging at him. It was the very thing that had kept him awake. The thing that had sent him down the corridor at dead of night, past the room where the Snitch lurked in his red contact lenses…

Of course! He sat up, with a jolt, banging his knee against the desk. Now he remembered! It was obvious. They should have spotted it. He *had* spotted it. He just hadn't quite got around to putting two and two together. And even if he had…

Even if he had, he wasn't sure he would have believed it. Not Miss Beam! Beautiful

Miss Beam! But Miss Beam had gone. Just as Mr Potts had gone. And Mr Hodge, before him. The evidence spoke for itself.

At the front of the class, Mr Trout droned on. Harry could hardly contain his impatience. The minute the bell rang, almost before Mr Trout had even left the room, the words came tumbling out of him.

'I've got it!'

'Got what?' said Joe.

'It was the chips! *The chips* … they all had this thing about chips!'

There was a pause.

'Who did?' said Ryan.

'Mr Hodge? Remember? Used to bring bags of them into class? Mr Potts? Complained he was eating too many? Said they made him fat? Miss Beam – '

'Miss Beam didn't get fat,' said Bal. They all sighed.

'No, but Harry's right. She did like her chips.' Joe said it regretfully. 'Remember that time with your gran and granddad?'

'Gorging herself on chips.'

Bal had turned very red. 'Miss Beam didn't *gorge*.'

'She was tucking into them, though. A huge great plateful.'

'Yeah, and remember when we did those essays and she said there were some aliens might consider chips a delicacy?'

'Doesn't prove anything!' said Bal.

Except that Miss Beam had disappeared, just like the others. Mr Potts had had a nervous breakdown. Mr Hodge … what had happened to Mr Hodge?

'Got took ill,' said Joe. 'Just suddenly. Least,' he added, 'that's what we was told.'

Bal scowled. He muttered again about it not proving anything, but the undeniable fact was that Miss Beam had gone. Back to her home planet, wherever that might be.

The next lesson was English. Year 6 waited, glumly, to see who would be taking it.

Probably the Head Master, thought Harry. He pulled a face. Dr Dredge was strict and stern with absolutely no sense of humour whatsoever. As different as could be from beautiful Miss Beam.

Year 6 braced themselves for the worst. Great was their surprise when the door opened and a totally new teacher walked in. He was young, with ginger hair and a long, forbidding beak of a nose. But he seemed friendly enough.

'Good morning, Year 6! My name is Mr Smith and I'm your new English teacher. I'm sure you must all be missing Miss Beam, I'm aware that she was very popular, but I'm here, now, and you must make the best of me. Just as I must make the best of you! I give you my word, I will try not to disappoint. Righty-ho!'

He rubbed his hands together. 'Let's get cracking! I've been reading some of the essays you did for Miss Beam on the subject of Unidentified Flying Objects. Most interesting! I think over the coming weeks we might explore the subject a bit further, if that's agreeable to you?'

Year 6 blinked. A teacher who actually asked if something was agreeable to them?

'What do you think?' said Mr Smith. 'A good idea, or not?'

'Good!' shouted Year 6.

'Of course, we'll have to do some curriculum work, as well. Set books, and all that. Literacy, and so forth. But that's all right! We'll fit it in. Just not too much of it. All work and no play makes Fred a very dull boy!'

Greatly daring, Bal said, 'Isn't it Jack, sir?'

'Jack?' Mr Smith seemed puzzled.

'Dull boy, sir.'

'Oh! Yes. How silly of me! Makes *Jack* a dull boy. We wouldn't want that, would we? Never be bored, is my motto! I think we're all going to get on just fine.'

Year 6 thought so, too. With his tufty ginger hair and his big beaky nose, the new teacher might not be much to look at – unlike Miss Beam. Beautiful Miss Beam! – but he seemed pretty cool, for all that.

'Literacy today, UFOs tomorrow. How about it?'

Year 6 took out their literacy papers without a murmur. They could live with that!

When the bell rang for the end of class, Mr Smith was the first to pack up his books.

'Ah!' he said. 'Lunch! I've been looking forward to this all morning. What do you suppose will be on the menu? Any chance of chips?' He licked his lips. 'I've been told they're really good!'

Innocently, Joe said, 'Do you like chips, sir?'

'Oh, I think so,' said Mr Smith. 'From what I've heard... yes! I'm sure I like chips. They're said to be a real delicacy! Do you find them a real delicacy?'

'When we're allowed to have 'em,' said Joe. 'Doesn't happen very often.'

'Oh.' Mr Smith's face fell.

'But you can get 'em down in the village.'

'Really? That's good to know. Maybe I should go down there right now. What do you think?'

Joe said, 'I think you should, sir. Be better than school dinners. Miss Beam used to go down there all the time.'

'In that case,' said Mr Smith, 'say no more! What was good enough for Miss Beam is good enough for me. See you later, boys!'

They watched as Mr Smith beetled off down the corridor.

'Guess that proves it,' said Bal. But he didn't sound as if he minded quite so much as he had before.

'Know what I reckon?' said Joe, as they made their way to the dining hall. 'I reckon we got it wrong about aliens. It's not them that's weird, it's all the rest of 'em!'

They gazed round the hall. They saw Mrs Jellybaby, staggering under the weight of all her beads and bangles. Mr Bulstrode, spluttering over his macaroni cheese. Mr O'Hooligan, Mr McNutter, Monsieur Tittinbot, screaming by the serving hatch. '*Attention, attention*! Watch out for the eye!'

'Mad,' said Joe. 'They're all mad!'

And *they* were the human beings. The alien was down in the village, eating chips.

'I reckon this one's gonna be OK,' said Joe.

'Reckon he is,' agreed Harry.

Just wait till he told Granddad! *There's this alien takes us for English…*

Gran, of course, wouldn't believe a word of it.

Jean Ure

*"I was caught in a transporter beam!"*

Jake is delighted when he's abducted by aliens.
Better still, they want him to carry out an
important mission. The world is in danger, and he
can help save it! The only problem is, the aliens
have taken his annoying sister Rosie too – and she
doesn't believe in aliens...

£4.99    ISBN 978 14081 1155 0

**Black Cats**
**Books to pounce on**

Sam Hay

*"We'd inherited a business. Maybe we were millionaires!"*

Albert Grub has an ordinary life until his dad inherits the famous Piddler's Porridge factory. But the town's noodle tycoon is keen to get his hands on the place. Is he after the legendary Spoon of Doom, supposed to be hidden in the factory? And what can Albert do to stop him?

£4.99    ISBN 978 14081 2399 7

Black Cats
Books to pounce on

Simon Cheshire

# DEADLINE

*"It was just gone six in the morning when the back door of Sam's house was kicked in."*

When Sam and Karen's mum is dragged away by armed police, their whole lives change. With no clues apart from a cryptic message screamed as she leaves, the kids find themselves in a dangerous race against time to stop a bomb from exploding and save their mum's life!

£4.99    ISBN 978 14081 3110 7

Black Cats
**Books to pounce on**